MW01504227

VAL WRIGHT is sixty-four years old and has been a vegetarian for over thirty years. She has loved books from a very early age and reads something every day. She taught yoga for twenty years and still practises at home. She now spends a few hours a week doing secretarial work for a local training company.

# THE BOOK OF PERI-RHYMES
## FOR LITTLE PEOPLE

# THE BOOK OF PERI-RHYMES
## FOR LITTLE PEOPLE

Val Wright

ATHENA PRESS
LONDON

THE BOOK OF PERI-RHYMES FOR LITTLE PEOPLE
Copyright © Val Wright 2008

## All Rights Reserved

ISBN: 978 1 84748 329 4

First published 2008 by
ATHENA PRESS
Queen's House, 2 Holly Road
Twickenham TW1 4EG
United Kingdom

Printed for Athena Press

# CONTENTS

# PERI AND THE HONEY BEE

P eri was a pixie
    Who lived in a magic wood.
He helped his many woodland friends
As often as he could.

His home he made beneath the roots
Of a very old oak tree.
Carpets were of soft, sheep's wool
And given to him free.

Furniture was from acorns made,
The walls were polished bark;
The entrance you would never find,
Especially in the dark.

One sunny morning, Peri woke
And jumped out of his bed.
'I fancy mushrooms for my tea,'
This cheerful pixie said.

So after breakfast he went out,
Carrying his load.
He took a basket and a knife
And walked the woodland road.

The wood was full of creatures –
Tiny, big and small.
Peri sang as he walked along,
Said 'Good morning' to them all.

The birds sang out on every tree,
The flowers faced the sun;
Squirrels and rabbits ran about
Enjoying all the fun.

But Peri hurried and did not stop,
He had no time to waste.
He had to get back home again –
Those mushrooms he could taste!

In the thickest part of the magic wood,
The finest mushrooms grew.
They were white and big and fat,
So only the best would do.

He cut some mushrooms with his knife,
His basket on the ground,
When suddenly, from somewhere near,
He heard a buzzing sound.

'Whatever's that?' poor Peri cried.
'I'm sure I'm on my own!'
But then he looked and he did see
He was not all alone.

Stuck in a sticky spider web
Was Buzz, his friend, the bee,
And however Buzz did turn and twist
He just could not get free.

The bee was getting angry,
His face had gone all red.
'Hang on there, Buzz, I've got a
  knife,'
Was all that Peri said.

The blade did cut the web to bits,
The bee was free at last.
He thanked the pixie gratefully,
The danger in the past.

Buzz said he would repay his friend
Although he had no money;
So Peri had mushrooms for his lunch
And for his tea had honey!

# PERI AND THE GNOME TWINS

The magic wood was dark and dull,
A shade of grey the sky.
Peri the Pixie shook his head
And gave a long, deep sigh.

'It looks like rain today,' he said.
'It's no fun out of doors.
I'll get to work at once, I think,
And do some household chores.'

With his many dusters bright
And polish, mop and broom,
He worked away without a break
To clean up every room.

Furniture and windows shone,
This now was plain to see,
But he was tired and had to rest
With a cup of acorn tea.

'I'll risk the rain and get some air,
That dust's gone up my nose!'
So Peri thought he'd have a walk
And changed his dusty clothes.

Outside, the sky got darker still,
It seemed like it was night.
He walked so far that very soon
His house was out of sight.

'I've walked too far!' the pixie cried.
'And now it starts to rain!'
It looked as if he would get wet
And ruin his clothes again.

Head down, he then began to run,
The rain came thick and fast.
Peri now was soaking wet
And hoped it would not last.

As he then ran around a tree,
He bumped into something there.
As he fell down and then looked up,
The sight did make him stare.

Two faces looked right down at him,
Both were just the same.
He thought that he had bumped his head
And that this was to blame.

But then he recognised the pair:
The gnome twins, Nip and Nap.
They pulled him to his feet at once
And gave his back a slap.

'Well, I never!' Nip exclaimed.
'It's Peri, without a doubt.'
'Come home with us,' Nap offered then,
'And we will dry you out!'

The three then hurried to the house.
They opened up the door
And fetched wet Peri a change of clothes,
Which they had in their store.

A pot of acorn tea was made;
They all sat round the fire.
They talked and laughed and swapped
   their news
As the warming flames leapt higher.

Peri's clothes were drying well,
Spread out upon a seat.
The twins said that it now was time
To have a bite to eat.

Home-made mushroom soup there was,
Followed by blackberry pie,
And by the time the meal was done
All Peri's clothes were dry.

The rain had stopped, the sun came out,
He started on his way.
He thanked his kind and thoughtful hosts
And would return one day.

A happy pixie walked back home
And, when he went to bed,
Happy thoughts of his twin friends
Whirled round inside his head.

# PERI AND THE MAGIC MIRROR

'Oh, not another dreary day,'
Peri the Pixie cried.
'I must go out and have a walk —
It's much too hot inside.'

He put on his hat and left the house.
The air was warm and damp.
'I bet it's dark in the heart of the
    wood.
I should have brought a lamp.'

Suddenly, there in the gloom,
Among the tall, green grass,
He spotted something hidden –
It looked like coloured glass.

A pretty mirror lay right there
In a fancy golden case.
Peri looked both hard and fast
But could not see his face.

'I do not understand at all.
The glass has a pearly sheen,
But nothing does reflect in it.
It's the strangest thing I've seen!'

Into his pocket the mirror went,
Not to leave it on the ground.
He would ask everyone he met
Until the owner was found.

None of the woodland creatures
Knew who owned the find,
But all would do their very best
To keep the fact in mind.

Then Fluff the Rabbit came along,
Who was questioned just the same.
'It belongs to a wizard,' she shyly said.
'A Mr Jinks by name.

'I have often seen him with it
And I heard that it was lost.
I know he's very angry
Because of what it cost.'

'Mr Jinks lives miles away,'
Peri then replied.
'I'll never get it back to him.
He'll think I have not tried.'

'Flash the Hare may take you there,'
The rabbit had a thought.
So with this latest task in hand,
The hare was duly sought.

Flash did agree to do the job
So, with Peri on his back,
He raced quickly through the magic
   wood
And along the mountain track.

The wizard's home was hidden well
Behind a clump of trees.
The pair did manage to get in,
But not with style or ease.

They made Mr Jinks very happy
And he patted Peri's head.
'You're an honest little fellow,'
The delighted wizard said.

'This was stolen by two goblins –
Nab and Grab just helped themselves;
But they must have dropped it in the
   wood
When chased by all my elves.

'It's valuable to only me;
No one knows its worth.
Through it I can see and speak
With all wizards around the earth.'

He then took from his magic chest
A small, silver chain and bell.
He placed it around the pixie's neck
And said, 'It will serve you well.'

Flash and Peri started back
For they had far to go.
As they entered the dark, dark wood,
The bell began to glow.

A dazzling light shone out from it
To lead them on their way.
Its light did get them safely home
From their adventure day.

# PERI HAS A LETTER

Peri the Pixie's asleep in bed
    When there's a *rat-tat-tat*.
He's now awake and quite alarmed
And says, 'Whatever's that?'

The noise, it came from his front door.
He took a little peek
And saw it was the woodpecker, Rap,
Knocking with his beak.

He was the woodland postman
Out early on the trail
With a big surprise for Peri,
For he had got some mail.

He made a cup of acorn tea
While opening the letter.
When he had read it, he did smile,
The day was getting better!

It was from one of Peri's friends –
A pixie, name of Blink.
'I have not seen him for some
    time –
At least five years, I think.'

The letter held some super news,
For Blink lived by the sea.
He said if Peri would visit him,
How happy he would be!

'A holiday by the sea!' he cried.
'I think that would be great.'
And there and then wrote back to Blink
So they could set a date.

There were a lot of things to do,
As well as pack a case.
The speed that Peri rushed around,
You'd think it was a race!

He wished to take a gift for Blink
That's not found by the sea.
Then he thought of taking honey
So he asked his friend the bee.

He would also take some mushrooms
And blackberries from the wood.
He knew just where the best ones grew;
They always were so good.

But there was one big problem:
Travelling to Blink's house.
He did not know just what to do
Till he met Max the Mouse.

'Ask Igor the Eagle,' Max said at once.
So Peri told creatures one and all
That he wished to speak to Igor,
If he was kind enough to call.

At a later date a message came,
Delivered by an elf.
He said, 'Igor is busy
Or he would have come himself.

'He will take you on your journey
And will pick you up at eight.
The sky gets very busy
If you start off rather late.'

The big day came, the weather was fine,
Peri stood by his gate.
Suddenly, Igor swooped right down,
Just on the dot of eight.

The eagle eyed the suitcase
That was clutched in Peri's hand.
'I hope that's not too heavy,
It makes it difficult to land.'

'You must not worry,' Peri said.
'My case is really light.
I hope you know the way to
  Blink's
And we get there all right.'

'I think I'll manage,' Igor replied.
'It's hard to miss the sea.'
Then Peri got excited
And kept shouting out with glee.

The eagle slowly turned his head
And then looked down his beak.
'Why are you making so much noise?
You chatter, shout and shriek.'

'I'm really sorry,' Peri said.
'You're usually alone,
But I am so excited —
It's the first time I have flown.'

The eagle smiled and flapped his wings;
Higher and higher he flew.
'Look out, Blink!' the pixie yelled.
'We're on our way to you!'

# PERI GOES SAILING

Peri is staying by the sea
  With Blink, his pixie friend,
And having days of fun and sun
Is what they do intend.

Blink's home is high up in a cliff –
A cave that's warm and dry.
From there he can look out to sea
And see the ships go by.

The pair walk on the sandy beach
And swim in the blue sea.
They gather lots of pretty shells
And chatter endlessly.

One day they go out in Blink's boat,
Which really is quite small;
Sailing out across the bay,
The waves look very tall.

'We are drifting out to sea,'
Says Peri with dismay.
'Don't worry at all,' Blink then replies,
'We'll soon be on our way.'

But really Blink was showing off;
The current was too strong.
The shore was fading very fast
As the boat was pushed along.

The pixies now were panicking;
The boat just would not turn.
Blink thought that sailing was easy,
But he had a lot to learn.

Suddenly they hear a shout
And Peri turns around.
'There's someone in the sea!' he cries.
'Surely she will drown!'

Blink then looked and laughed out loud.
'I think help is at hand.
That's Coral, she's a mermaid.
She will get us back to land.'

The mermaid swam around the boat
And waved her shiny tail.
She said, 'My friends will help you now.
You just control the sail.

'Meet Splish and Splash, my dolphin
   friends.
We'll push with all our might
Until you're back inside the bay
And the beach is back in sight.'

The dolphins nudged, the mermaid
   pushed,
The boat turned to the shore.
The pixies thanked the helpful friends;
Glad to be safe once more.

The dolphins smiled and swam away.
Coral waved a hand.
Blink and Peri pulled the boat
On to the fine, white sand.

That evening, sitting in Blink's cave
Beside a driftwood fire,
They drank a pot of seaweed tea,
But quickly they did tire.

They fell into their comfy beds
And sleepily did say,
Although they had been very scared,
It had been a fantastic day!

# THE PIXIES AND THE DRAGON

'**I**'d love to live here by the sea,'
Peri said one day.
'Well then,' said Blink, 'you're welcome,
If you wish to stay.

'I think you'd miss your woodland friends.
The sea is just a change,
But if you really want to move
It's easy to arrange.

'Don't forget it's summer now,
The winter's not so nice.
It can get windy and so cold,
Though there's no snow or ice.'

'I guess you're right,' Peri did agree.
'There are different things to do,
So if I lived here all the time
It would get ordinary too!'

'I tell you what,' Blink had a thought,
'Let's walk into the town.
There are some things I need to buy,
So now I'll write them down.

'The weather's not so warm today –
It's windy by the sea.
We'll go and do this shopping
And get something nice for tea.'

The pair walked around the many shops
And the market run by elves.
Peri bought gifts for all his friends,
Then they did treat themselves.

Fresh fruit for tea and sticky buns
Were on their shopping list.
Teacakes to toast were next to buy –
They must not be missed.

Loaded down with many bags,
The pixies walked back home.
'We are tired and hungry with aching feet,'
They both were heard to groan.

'Let's light the fire,' Blink said at once,
'So we can have some tea.'
They found some wood and set to work,
But it was not to be.

The wood was damp and would not light.
Blink looked out through the door.
He said, 'There's driftwood on the beach.
We'll go and get some more!'

Though they were tired and hungry still,
The pixies walked to the beach,
But all the wood was soaking wet
That was within their reach.

They turned around to go back home
But, much to their surprise,
They passed a cave high in the cliff
From which some smoke did rise.

'That cave's on fire!' Peri cried,
But Blink just shook his head.
'Scorch the Dragon now lives there.
He's breathing fire,' he said.

Peri looked scared and Blink did laugh,
'He really is quite small
And, though he is a dragon,
He is not fierce at all.'

Just then, the dragon left the cave
And saw the pixie pair,
But before he could put the fire out
The flames had singed their hair.

'I am so sorry,' the dragon said,
'But I must practise with my flame.
For a dragon, I am not fierce enough
And my friends think I'm too tame.

'WHY ARE YOU ON THE BEACH SO LATE?
IT IS NOT VERY LIGHT.'
The pixies sat upon a rock
And told him of their plight.

The dragon thought, then gave a grin.
He told them of his plan.
He said, 'I LL TAKE YOU BOTH BACK NOW,
AND HELP YOU IF I CAN.'

The pixies jumped upon his back;
They flew to Blink's front door.
The dragon stayed outside the cave
And then began to roar.

The flames he made were large and hot.
'THE BEST YET!' Scorch did boast.
His plan right now was very plain
As the teacakes he did toast.

All three sat down and ate the meal.
The teacakes tasted good.
Scorch helped out his friends once more
And dried the firewood.

He said goodnight and flew back home.
The pixies went to bed.
*I've had another super day,*
Was the last thought in Peri's head.

# PERI GOES HOME

To say goodbye to his new friends
Peri had to do:
Coral and her dolphin pals
And Scorch the Dragon too.

One morning, early, Igor came
And waited at Blink's gate,
But Peri was not ready yet
So then he had to wait.

'Don't look so grumpy,' Peri said
As he rushed through the door.
'Here's a present — a silver ring
To wear around your claw.'

The eagle flew up in the sky;
The pixie held on tight.
Over hills and fields they went,
Then the wood came into sight.

As they at last reached Peri's house,
His friends were standing round,
And the tree which held his little home
Lay flat upon the ground.

'Whatever's happened to my house?'
Cried Peri in dismay.
'Everything I had is lost
Since I have been away.'

'The wicked goblins are to blame,'
Fluff the Rabbit said.
'They stole some spells from Mr Jinks
As he lay in his bed.

'They used his magic to make a storm,
Which then blew down your tree.
It fell upon both Nab and Grab
And they could not get free.

'He has locked them in his magic tower
Until they do behave.
He will not let them out just yet,
Although they rant and rave.

'But this has happened for the best –
Your tree was old and dead.
It could have happened while you slept
And fallen on your head!'

'You can stay with us,' Nip said at once,
'Till you find another home.'
'You know you're always welcome,'
Said Nap, the other gnome.

# PERI'S NEW HOME

P eri stayed with Nip and Nap,
  But could not sleep a wink.
'Why ever did I come back home?
I should have stayed with Blink.'

The gnome twins brought him tea in bed
And cooked his favourite food,
But Peri never seemed to be
In a very happy mood.

Then Fluff the Rabbit came one day
And said, 'You've a new house.
It's better than the other –
It was found by Max the Mouse.

'Mr Jinks has made a spell
To strengthen this new tree,
So if you can get ready now
We will go and see!'

Fluff led the three along a path
To the middle of the wood.
She stopped in a small clearing
Where a massive oak tree stood.

They all climbed down inside the tree
And walked and looked around
'It's brilliant!' Peri said at last.
'Just look what Max has found.

'I cannot wait to move in here —
It is so big and light.
Lots of space and nice and dry,
Everything's just right.'

The friends said that they all would help
To clean and decorate.
A very excited Peri said
He thought that would be great.

'Mr Jinks has stored your furniture,'
Fluff was heard to say.
'When you need it, tell his elves.
They'll bring it right away.'

The next day saw the friends at work.
New sheep's wool on the floors.
They washed the windows, cleaned the walls
And painted all the doors.

When this was done, the elves arrived
With tables, chairs and bed,
Books and lamps and curtains
And cushions in bright red.

Peri's home was a cheerful sight,
His delight was plain to see.
He thanked his friends and all the elves
And made them stay to tea.

He realised how kind they were
And was ashamed to think
That he had thought of leaving them
To go and live with Blink.

# PERI HAS AN IDEA

Peri's in his brand-new home.
It all is bright and clean.
He thought about his woodland friends,
How helpful they had been.

He wanted to repay them all,
But how he did not know.
Everyone worked very hard
As his finished house did show.

He thought and thought for quite a while
As he sipped some acorn tea.
Then, jumping to his feet, he said,
'An idea's come to me.

'I'll give a party for them all
And do everything just right.
I'll send out invitations.
We shall have a super night!'

He fetched some paper and a pen
To write down every guest.
'They'll have a treat they won't
  forget,
'Cause they deserve the best.'

'There's Max the Mouse, Flash the
  Hare,
Nip and Nap and Fluff,
Mr Jinks and all his elves:
I think that is enough.'

All the letters were sent out
For two weeks from that date.
Peri was eager to thank his friends;
It seemed so long to wait.

He then began to write a list
Of things to buy and do.
It seemed he may need three whole weeks
Instead of only two!

# PERI'S PARTY

The party day was here at last,
Peri had worked for hours.
His tree house looked so beautiful,
Decked in fairy lights and flowers.

Drinks and glasses stood in rows
With delicious things to eat.
The table was piled very high
With both savoury and sweet.

Easy chairs around the room
All had cushions bright;
Little lamps in corners gave
A soft and glowing light.

One by one, his friends arrived,
Just as the sky grew dark.
*'This room is like a picture,'*
A guest was heard to remark.

Coats were taken at the door
Then drinks were handed round,
But suddenly, in all the noise,
They heard a cheerful sound.

Nip and Nap had brought their fiddles
And did play a merry tune,
Which meant that all the other guests
Were dancing pretty soon.

The evening got very lively
With food and drink going fast.
Peri looked a little worried,
Hoping they both would last.

Hot and tired from dancing,
They all did take a seat
And sang some favourite pixie songs
While resting aching feet.

When all the songs were over,
Mr Jinks took the floor
To do some amazing magic tricks
Never seen before.

The party went on for some hours
Well into the night
And slowly it came to an end
As it was getting light.

The friends thanked Peri one by one,
They'd all enjoyed themselves,
And everyone was taken home
By Mr Jinks and the elves.

The magician had a magic sleigh
Big enough for all to ride.
There was Nip and Nap, Fluff and Flash
And Max the Mouse inside.

With just one word from Mr Jinks,
The sleigh flew through the sky.
Over the side they looked below
And saw Peri wave goodbye.

So happy in his brand-new home,
He had no time to think,
But realised, without a doubt,
That he should write to Blink.

He must repay his kindly friend,
Inviting him to stay.
Maybe in the cold winter months
When the seaside's cold and grey.

His thoughts then turned to Nab and Grab,
Which made him start to smile.
For they now worked for Mr Jinks
And must do for a while.

He makes them both work very hard,
Attending to his needs,
Until they have been made to pay
For all their wicked deeds.

Peri stood in the magic wood,
Looking at the starry night,
And was so pleased that after all
Everything had turned out right!

Printed in the United Kingdom
by Lightning Source UK Ltd.
134763UK00001B/164/P